Sleeping Beauty
and Other Classic
Fairy Tales

igloobooks

The Princess and the Pea

Once, there was a handsome prince who wanted to find a princess to marry. He had met many princesses on his travels, but had yet to fall in love.

Then, one dark, stormy night, there was a **knock** on the palace door.

The king **hurried** to see who it was.

At the door stood a young girl, wet through from the heavy rain. **"Good heavens,"** said the king.

"I am a princess," she said. "Can you help me? I got lost in this horrid storm and need shelter."

"Of course," said the king. **"Do come inside."**

Inside, the queen overheard. She wanted to
know if the girl was a real princess, as she claimed.

**"Put one pea at the bottom
of twenty mattresses,"**
the queen commanded
her servants.

Soon, the task was complete
and it was time for bed.

In the morning, the king and queen
asked the girl how she'd slept.

"**Badly!**" she replied.
"It felt like I was lying on something hard."

The queen was delighted. Only a true princess
would feel a single pea beneath twenty soft mattresses.
The queen decided to introduce her to the prince.

When he saw the princess, the prince fell in love with her. At last he had found a princess to marry.

The king and queen were very happy, too. In fact, they even kept the pea, as a reminder of the day their son finally found a wife.

Cinderella

Long ago, there lived a beautiful girl who had a wicked stepmother and two spiteful stepsisters. They took all her nice clothes and left her with just a ragged, old dress.

"That's all you need for cleaning and cooking," said the cruel stepmother.

One day, a special invitation arrived. **"It's for the royal ball!"** cried the stepmother. **"You must help us to prepare,"** she ordered Cinderella.

The stepmother and stepsisters left for the ball.
"Oh, how I wish I could go," sobbed Cinderella.

POOF! A shining figure appeared.

"I am your fairy godmother and you shall go to the ball," she said.

In a **flash** of light, the fairy godmother turned mice, rats and a pumpkin into footmen, horses and a glowing carriage. Then, Cinderella found that she was wearing a **shimmering** ball gown.

"**Go to the ball**," said the fairy godmother, "**but beware. The magic ends at midnight.**"

When Cinderella entered the ballroom, everyone gasped. The prince, captivated by his **beautiful** guest, asked her to dance.

All night long, Cinderella and the prince danced together.

Then, the clock struck twelve. **"I must go!"** cried Cinderella.

"Wait!" cried the prince, but Cinderella had gone.

All that was left was a single glass slipper.

"When I find the girl whose foot fits this slipper, she shall be my wife," declared the prince.

The prince searched the kingdom. At Cinderella's house,
the slipper did not fit the stepsisters' feet.
"Who else lives here?" asked the prince.
"No one," lied the stepmother.

Suddenly, Cinderella **burst** into the room.

"**I do!**" she cried.

Sure enough, the slipper was a **perfect** fit.

The prince asked Cinderella to marry him and she accepted. She forgave her stepmother and stepsisters, but they were so jealous, they left the town and never came back.

After that, Cinderella **never** wore rags again. She was a real princess and lived happily ever after with her **handsome** prince.

Sleeping Beauty

Long ago, a princess was born. The whole kingdom celebrated and two magical fairies gave her gifts of beauty and kindness.

Suddenly, an **evil** fairy appeared. **"You forgot to invite me!"** she screeched and she cursed the princess.

"On her fifteenth birthday, she will prick her finger on a spindle and **die.***"*

She disappeared and a third fairy spoke.
"I cannot undo the curse," she said, "but the princess
will not die. She will sleep for one hundred years."

Time passed and the princess grew to be beautiful and kind. On the morning of her fifteenth birthday the princess explored the castle.

She found a set of stairs and **tiptoed** up the steps.

At the top was a door with a key in the lock.

The princess turned the key and opened the door.
Inside, an old woman sat at a spindle.

"What are you doing?"
asked the princess.

"I am spinning," replied the woman. "Come and try."

No sooner had the princess touched the spindle, than
she pricked her finger and fell into a deep sleep.

Soon, the whole palace was under a

spell of sleep.

The horse slept in the courtyard. The dog slept by the fire.

Even the king and queen slept on their thrones.

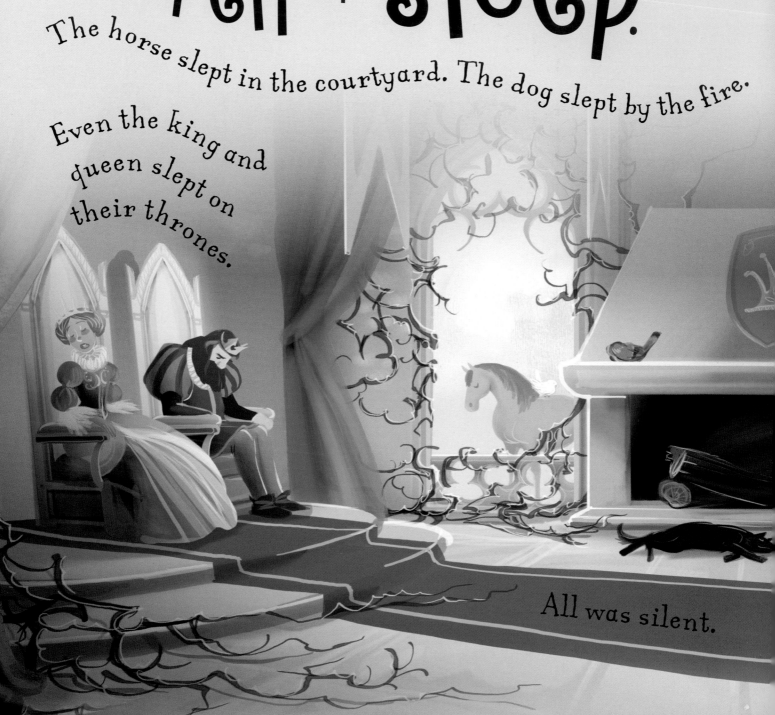

All was silent.

As time drifted by, the palace became covered in a tangle of thorns.

One hundred years passed. Then, one day, a prince
came to the enchanted palace.

He drew his **SWORD** and began to **cut** at the thorns.

As if by magic, the thorns parted. The prince
stepped into the silent courtyard.

Soon, the prince came across where the princess was sleeping. "So, **you are Sleeping Beauty**," he said.

The prince knelt down to **kiss** her. As he did so, the princess woke up.

She looked at him so sweetly that he instantly fell in **love** with her.

At that moment, the spell was **lifted** and everybody woke up. The sleeping palace had come back to life.

The prince and princess were to be married and everyone lived

happily ever after.